CW00956417

Save the Pitch

Other titles in the same series

Ghost Goalie
The Tigers football team are full of confidence about the next match. But their coach falls ill just before they are due to play! The Tigers are desperate. How can they win without him? Perhaps they can, with a very special bit of ghostly help . . .

The Terrible Trainer
The Tigers football team have a substitute coach, but he is mean and shouts a lot. He makes the Tigers feel awful. How can they get rid of Mr Bawl and find a coach who will make sure they can win?

The Cup Final
The Tigers football team have to win this last game to win the Cup! But disaster strikes when their coach's head becomes stuck in some iron railings when trying to get the ball. What can they do to save the match?

Tigers on Television
The Tigers football team have a nail-biting match to play, and a local TV crew has come to film them in action. But the TV cameras have a terrible effect on the team's ghost trainer and he can't coach them properly! What can the Tigers do?

Ghost Striker
The Tigers football team are facing a difficult away match against a tough team, but they have got the special help of their ghost goalie . . . or have they? Things look bad when an old opponent arrives – intent on revenge!

Save the Pitch

J. BURCHETT AND S. VOGLER

ILLUSTRATED BY Guy Parker-Rees

BLOOMSBURY

LONDON BERLIN NEW YORK

For Katie and Jennifer Burchett

Bloomsbury Publishing, London, Berlin and New York

First published in Great Britain in 1998 by Bloomsbury Publishing Plc
36 Soho Square, London, W1D 3QY
This edition published in July 2010

Text copyright © Janet Burchett and Sara Vogler 1998
Illustrations copyright © Guy Parker-Rees 1998
The moral rights of the author and illustrator have been asserted

All rights reserved
No part of this publication may be reproduced or
transmitted by any means, electronic, mechanical, photocopying
or otherwise, without the prior permission of the publisher

A CIP catalogue record of this book is available from the British Library

ISBN 978 1 4088 0827 6

FSC
Mixed Sources
Product group from well-managed
forests and other controlled sources
Cert no. SGS-COC-2061
www.fsc.org
© 1996 Forest Stewardship Council

Printed in Great Britain by Clays Ltd, St Ives plc, Bungay, Suffolk

1 3 5 7 9 10 8 6 4 2

www.bloomsbury.com/childrens

Save The Pitch

Billy Bright and the Tigers
Under-Tens Football Team
were practising hard in
Tottingham Town Park.
Tomorrow they were playing
the Colts. It was the last game
of the season. If the Tigers won

they would go top of the Junior
Football League. There was
only one problem. Their coach,
Billy's dad, had fallen over the

ball. Mum was sliding him into the back of the car with the help of two park keepers.

'Ow!' he groaned. 'My back.'

'What about tomorrow's game?' asked Blocker. 'We need a coach.'

'Yeah, we're useless without a coach,' said Rick. 'We argue.'

'We all go for the ball,' said Kim.

'We get into a right mess,' said Bullseye.

'Billy'll coach us,' said Rob, 'won't you, Billy?'

'Yes,' said Billy. 'I've got my coaching book at home.'

'No problem then,' said Mona the goalkeeper. 'We can win tomorrow.'

'We're the Tigers . . .' started Ellen.

'Hear us roar . . .' chanted Joe.

'SEVEN-NIL WILL BE THE SCORE!' shouted everyone.

Billy always took over when his dad couldn't coach. The

Tigers thought Billy and his book were great. But Billy had a secret. He didn't really have a coaching book. He had help from Springer Spannell – Tottingham Town's most famous goalkeeper. But only Billy could see Springer.

Springer Spannell was . . . a ghost!

Springer would know the Tigers needed him. But there was no sign of him yet. 'We're ready, Coach,' said Terry. Billy had no choice. He had to coach the team until Springer turned up.

'Er . . . knee-bends,' said Billy. 'A hundred and fifty.'

'All right,' said Billy.
'Tackling instead.'

But the Tigers ended up in a
heap.

'Call that tackling?' said a
voice.

Billy spun round. A man stood
there grinning.

The man was wobbly round

the edges. And Billy could see right through him. It was like looking through a pineapple jelly. It was Springer Spannell! 'You're here at last,' whispered Billy.

PHANTOMS IN FOOTBALL (PHJFA) RULES
RULE SEVEN: A GHOST COACH CAN ONLY APPEAR TO ONE MEMBER OF THE TEAM, AND IF ANYONE ELSE FINDS OUT THE COACH GETS THE SACK

'I was lucky to get out of that alive,' growled Blocker. 'Not you, Blocker,' sighed Billy.

Billy wished he could tell the team about Springer. It would be much easier. But if Billy told anyone, the ghost goalie would disappear for ever. It was in his PhIFA rules.

'Come on,' said Springer. 'Get them on the pitch and into a game. By the way, what's happened to Dad this time?'

'Hurt his back,' muttered Billy. 'Showing off. He was doing a tackle.'

'Tell him to lie flat,' said Springer, bounding on to the pitch.

As usual, Springer forgot he wasn't a goalie any more. He crouched next to Mona in the goalmouth. Billy groaned. Springer should be on the touchline. On the touchline, he could shout instructions to Billy and Billy could pass them on.

Billy beckoned to Springer.
Springer ignored him but half
the team came over.

'What do you want?'

'What's the matter?'

'Can't we start?'

'Not you lot,' sighed Billy. 'I
was just . . . um . . . warming

up my coaching finger! It's in the book.'

Billy tried whistling to Springer. 'Oh!' said Bullseye, tying his bootlace. 'Are we starting?' He tried to kick off, tripped on his lace and fell over. 'You could have waited, Coach!' 'You weren't supposed to kick off!' shouted Billy.

He went to get Springer out of goal. Lisa was passing to Rick. Rick ran with the ball towards the goal. Springer came forwards. He did a brilliant tackle. Well, it would have been brilliant if he hadn't been a ghost. The ball went straight through his boot. Billy waved wildly at Springer.

Rick scored easily.

'That wasn't fair,' said
Mona. 'I was watching Billy.'
'You should have been
watching the game,' said Rick.
'But Billy was waving!' shouted
Mona. 'He's turned into a
windmill,' laughed Kim.

Billy put his arms down.

'Just . . . er . . . warming up the coaching shoulders!' Springer came over.

'Sorry, lad,' he said. 'I forgot.' He went to the touchline. Play started again. This time it went well.

Suddenly there was a roar of engines. Two lorries and a digger drove up.

'Oi, you lot!' shouted a big workman. 'Clear off. We've got to dig here.' Billy couldn't believe his ears. Dig up their pitch!

'Ask him when,' said

Springer. 'You've got an important match tomorrow.'

'When?' asked Billy. 'We've got an important match tomorrow.' A little workman laughed.

'Not here, you haven't,' he sneered. 'We're laying new pipes – starting ten minutes ago! You heard what he said. Clear off!'

The Tigers were horrified.

'What are we going to do?' asked Mona.

'If we don't play tomorrow, we won't get the points,' said Rick.

'We won't go to the top of the league,' wailed Terry.

'Dad'll sort it out,' said Billy. 'I'll take Springer along . . . I mean . . . I'll spring along!'

Dad was peeling potatoes.

Billy told him the problem. Dad leapt into action. Well, he would have leapt into action if he hadn't been strapped to a door.

'I'll get you another pitch,' he said. 'Where's the phone? . . .

Hello? Sunflower School? Is
your pitch available tomorrow?
. . .You're having a Morris
dancing marathon. Thanks
anyway.' He dialled again.

'Hello? Tottingham Town
FC? Is your pitch free
tomorrow? . . . Oh, a

hang-gliding display. Thanks anyway.' He scratched his head.

'One last chance,' he said. 'I'll try the AA. Hello? Allotment Association? Is that little bit of ground by your potato patch free tomorrow?

. . . Marrow Juggling. All day?
. . . Thanks anyway.'

'You'll have to get your pitch
back,' said Springer.

'How can we get our pitch
back?' said Billy.

'I don't see how we can get
our pitch back by tomorrow,'

said Dad. Springer whipped out his rule book.

'Yes, you will,' he said. 'I'll find a way.'

'Yes, we will,' said Billy. 'He'll find a way.'

When they got back to the park, the digger was standing right at the touchline. But it was empty. The workmen were having a kick about.

'We'll show these kids some real football,' said the workman with the funny hat.

'I've got it!' shouted Springer, waving his book.

'You've got it?' exclaimed Billy.

'Got what?' asked Bullseye.

'Got what?' Billy asked Springer.

'Don't ask me!' said Bullseye.

'Rule number thirty-three,' read Springer. 'If a ghost coach – that's me – and his team – that's you – have anyone trying to stop a match – that's them – he can spook them out.'

'That's a brainwave,' said Billy.

'What is?' asked Mona.

'His brain's leaking,' laughed Rob.

'Whoooooooo!' moaned
Springer. He ran on to the
pitch, pulling horrible faces.

'Eeeeeeeee!' he shrieked. The
workmen took no notice.

'Aaaaaaaargh!' he wailed,
flapping his arms wildly at the
big workman. The big
workman ran straight through
him.

'It's hopeless,' said Billy.

'Why are you bothering to watch then?' said Terry.

'We're never going to get our pitch back,' sighed Bullseye. 'Let's go home.' The team picked up their kit.

'Wait!' said Billy. 'Something's happening.'

Something very odd was

happening to the ball. The
Tigers ran to the touchline.

'The ball's going up the pitch
– on its own!' gasped Joe. The
workmen gawped.

'Must be the slope of the
park,' said the big workman.

The ball dribbled three times

round the bald workman,
bounced off the skinny
workman's back, wiggled round
the goalie and thumped into the
back of the net.

'I didn't know you could do
that,' shouted Billy to Springer.
'Never touched it,' said the big
workman.

'Must be the wind,' said the little workman. 'Come on, let's play!'

'. . . N-n-n-not me,' said the big workman.

The others kicked off again. The workman with the tattoo dribbled round the goalie and took a shot at goal. The ball

flew towards the net . . . and stopped in mid-air.

'What a goalie!' gasped Billy.

'What goalie?' asked Mona. The ball bounced three times on the pitch and sailed off into the air.

'It's like there's an invisible goalie,' quavered the skinny workman.

'It's like there's a g-g-g-g-ghost!' stammered the bald workman. 'I d-d-d-don't like it.'

'The pitch is haunted!' shouted the big workman. 'We're not digging here.' And they fled.

The Tigers looked at each other.' Do you think there *is* a ghost?' said Terry.

'I'm not playing on a haunted pitch,' said Ellen.

'I can't tackle a spook!' howled Blocker.

'Tell them you did it,' said Springer.

'I did it,' said Billy.

'How?' demanded Kim.

'With . . . er . . . magnets and
a piece of elastic. It's in the
book.'

'Wow!' said the Tigers.

'That was brilliant, Springer!'
whispered Billy. 'But I thought
you couldn't touch a real ball.'

'Normally I can't,' said Springer. 'But PhIFA rule number thirty-four says – A ghost coach – that's me – can play with a real football when using rule thirty-three – that's the one before . . .'

'Springer!' interrupted Billy. 'What's happening? You're fading!'

'That's the only problem with rule thirty-four,' said Springer faintly. 'I disappear. I can't coach for six . . .'

'Six?' said Billy. 'Six what?' But Springer had vanished.

'Six minutes?' shouted Billy. 'Six years? Six what?'

'Six-nil, Coach,' said Rick.

'We'll score more than that,'

said Joe. 'We're the Tigers . . .'
'Hear us roar. SIXTEEN-NIL
WILL BE THE SCORE!'
shouted everyone.

'Yeah,' said Billy, trying to
smile. Supposing Springer was
gone for six centuries!

'Hello, Billy,' said Dad. 'Are
the workmen still there?'

'No,' said Billy glumly. 'They thought the pitch was haunted. They ran away.'

'Great!' said Dad. 'I was about to phone and cancel the match.' 'You might as well . . .' began Billy.

'You're sure to win tomorrow,' interrupted Dad.

'But Dad, we won't . . .'

'Who'd want to haunt a pitch like that!' chuckled Dad. Billy hoped the pitch *would* be haunted tomorrow – by Springer.

Billy barely tasted his tea. He hardly noticed what was on telly. He absentmindedly stepped over Dad. How could the Tigers win tomorrow without Springer?

That night, Billy had a dream. He was on the pitch at Wembley. It was Billy Bright v the Best Ever Footballers. Billy didn't stand a chance. The score was already ninety-nine-

nil. Springer was on the
touchline.

'Springer!' yelled Billy. 'Help
me!' 'Sorry lad,' shouted

Springer, 'You're on your own . . .' He disappeared.

Billy found he couldn't move. All around him the Allotment Association were planting marrows. And now the Best Ever Footballers had turned into man-eating tigers dressed as Morris dancers. They were hang-gliding towards him. They landed on him! Billy was crushed underneath a huge pile of . . . bedclothes. He sat bolt upright in bed. What if Springer had gone for ever?

It was Saturday. The Tigers ran out on to their pitch.

How was Billy going to coach the team? Dad couldn't

help. He couldn't shout because it hurt his back. And anyway, as he was still strapped to his board, he could only see the sky.

If only Springer was here. Billy wished the workmen had dug up the whole park!

'What's the matter, Coach?' said Joe.

'What about our pre-match talk?' asked Lisa.

'Er,' said Billy. 'Strikers, don't forget to . . . well . . . strike . . . and . . . er . . . midfield . . .'

'Tell them to remember one-touch passing,' said a voice. It was Springer!

'Go on then,' said Springer.

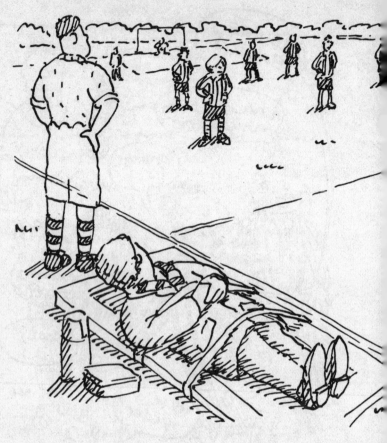

'Tell them, one-touch passing . . .'
   '. . . accurate throw-ins, and
go out to win!' Billy repeated.
The Tigers got into position. 'I
thought you'd gone for ever!'

said Billy. 'I told you – six hours,' said Springer. 'I'm only late now because someone's moved the town sundial.' He strode to the touchline.

The final match of the season started. The Colts were top of the league – by one point. The Tigers needed to win to overtake them. It was going to be a tough game.

Billy kicked off. The Colts were playing defensively. They wanted to hang on to the top position. They marked the Tigers tightly. Wherever Billy went, there was a defender glued to him. Each time he got into their half, he was tackled. 'Find space!' shouted Springer. He paced up and down the touchline.

But it was the Colts who found the first gap. Their main striker made a fast forward run. Blocker rushed in to jockey him but he was wrong-footed. The striker did a one-two with his partner and ran with the ball towards the goal. 'Tell Rob to get in there!' shouted Springer.

'Rob!' shouted Billy. 'Get in
there.' Rob blocked the striker's
path. The striker did a clever
back-heel pass to his partner
who walloped the ball at goal.

It took the defenders by surprise. The ball flashed past Mona's outstretched fingers and hit the back of the net. One-nil.

The Tigers launched a counter-attack. Bullseye kicked off to Billy. Billy sent a long, fast ball up to Joe who was on

the left wing. He crossed it to
Kim to pass to Bullseye. 'Tell
Kim to go for it!' yelled
Springer.

But Billy didn't need to. Kim
had seen her chance. She
volleyed the ball hard into the

Dad's hand knitted scarf

net. The crowd roared. Dad
waved his scarf. Springer
jiggled with excitement.

'Tell Blocker to stick with
that striker,' said Springer at
half time. 'Tell Kim to . . .'
Billy didn't get the chance. The

digger, at the side of the pitch, was starting up! 'They've come back!' yelled Blocker.

'What can we do?' asked Ellen.

'Lie on the pitch,' said Springer. 'Lie on the pitch,' said

Billy. 'They're not going to spoil our game.'

The digger roared. The shovel lifted. The Tigers covered their eyes.

And then – the digger reversed and moved away. Billy could see the big workman at the controls. He looked terrified. 'You can get up,' he shouted. 'I've only come to collect the equipment. I wouldn't dig there for a million pounds.' The Colts stared at the Tigers. 'Just resting,' called Billy.

The second half was full of tight marking and careful tackles. But the Tigers needed to attack. They needed another

goal. Billy ran with the ball. He
ran like the wind. He ran deep
into the Colts' half. Soon there
was only one defender between
him and the goal. He was just
outside the penalty area. It was
looking good.

'Man on!' shouted Springer.

wobble

Billy had seen the defender
coming up from behind. He
screened the ball but he was
brought down by a clumsy
tackle. The whistle blew. Free
kick to the Tigers. Billy got
ready. The Colts made a wall
in front of the goal.

'Banana kick!' yelled
Springer. Billy placed the ball
on the grass. He took a
measured run-up. He swerved

the ball round the defensive wall. It hit the post . . . and spun into the goal.

At the final whistle, the Tigers hugged each other. Dad punched the air. Springer ran round wildly, patting everyone on the back.

'Couldn't have done it without you,' Billy told Springer.

'Couldn't have done it without *you*, Coach,' said Rob.

'We're the Tigers, Hear us roar. TWO-OO ONE WAS THE FINAL SCORE!' chanted the winners of the Junior Football League.